REMY'S
BLUEPRINTS

By Sharon Leya | Art by Janne Maru

This book belongs to:

Special thanks to Leah Golub and Jessica Wachsman Selznick for their editorial and creative guidance.

Text copyright © Sharon Leya, 2023

Illustrations copyright © Art by Janne Maru, 2023

ISBN: 9798387340628

Remy was excited about her first day of school!

Earlier that morning, Mommy and Daddy had surprised her with a set of colorful building blocks to celebrate the special day ahead. Remy loved building with blocks.

Remy walked hand-in-hand with Mommy and Daddy through the neighborhood, looking at all the houses.

"Do you see that house?" Mommy asked. "Daddy and I were the architects who designed that house."

Remy knew that Mommy and Daddy were architects, which meant that they used their imagination to create all the instructions for how a house should be built, like what it would look like, where the doors and windows would go, and how tall it would be. Those instructions were called "blueprints."

Remy was very proud of Mommy and Daddy. She decided she was going to use her new building blocks to build a house for her baby doll as soon as she got home from school.

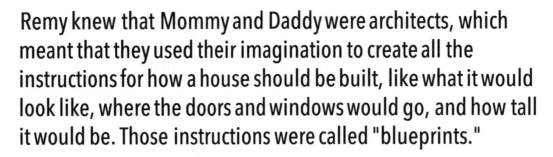

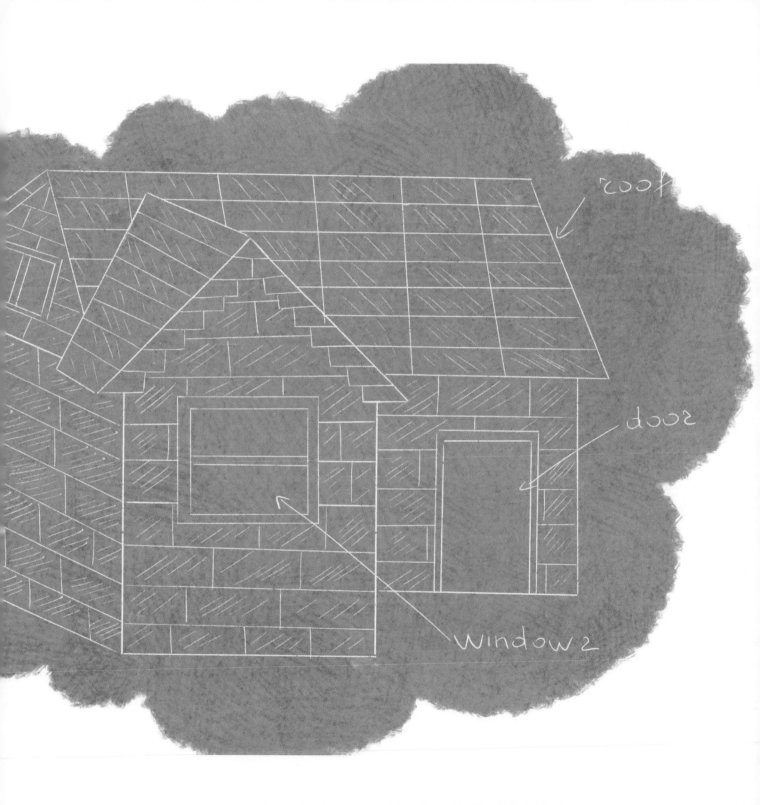

When Remy arrived at school, she saw her neighbor, Emmett, with his mommy and daddy.
"Guess what, Remy?" Emmett said.
"I have a new baby sister!" he said proudly.

"Wow!" Remy replied. "Can I come see your baby sister soon?"

"Of course!" said Emmett's daddy.

"Where did you get the baby?" asked Remy.

"My mommy and daddy said they made her with lots of love and a little bit of science," said Emmett.

"Cool!" said Remy. And then she began to think.

Later that day, after a wonderful first day of school, Remy rushed home to play with her blocks. But she knew she had one big question she needed answered.

"Mommy," she asked. "Did you and Daddy make me the same way Emmett's parents made his new baby sister?"

"We made you with a lot of love and a little bit of science, too," Mommy said. "But we also had some extra special help from two very kind people."

"What kind of special help?" Remy asked.

"Some people make a baby using donors," Mommy explained. "And that is how YOU were made."

"A donor? What is that?" Remy asked.

"A donor is a person who wants to help others grow their families," Daddy said.

"How do they do that?" Remy wondered.

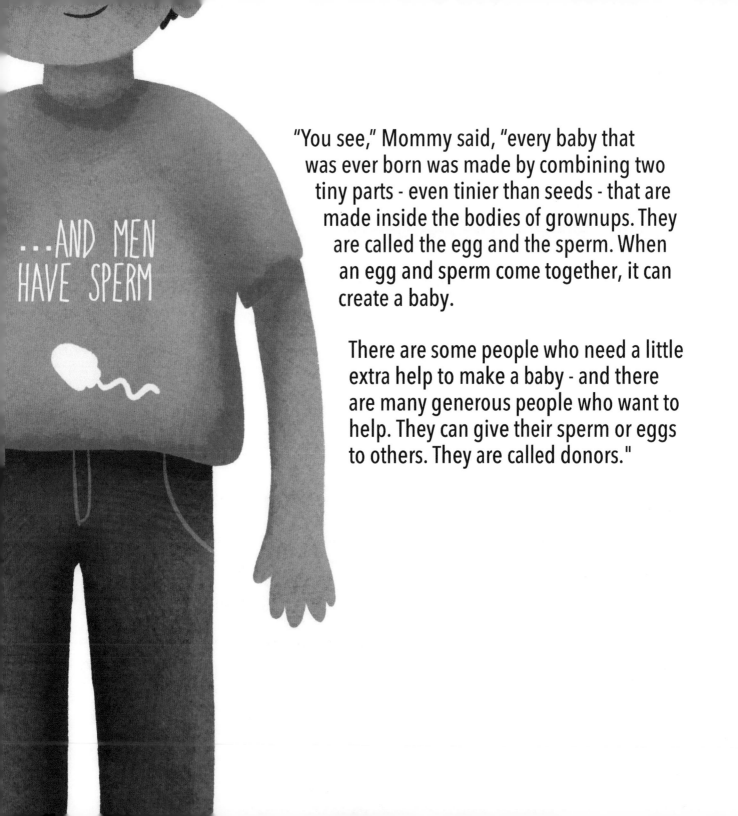

...AND MEN HAVE SPERM

"You see," Mommy said, "every baby that was ever born was made by combining two tiny parts - even tinier than seeds - that are made inside the bodies of grownups. They are called the egg and the sperm. When an egg and sperm come together, it can create a baby.

There are some people who need a little extra help to make a baby - and there are many generous people who want to help. They can give their sperm or eggs to others. They are called donors."

"When Daddy and I were ready to grow our family, we combined sperm from a donor with an egg from a donor and it turned into you!

You grew inside my uterus, which is like a cozy room right below my tummy where a baby can grow. And nine months later you were ready to be born."

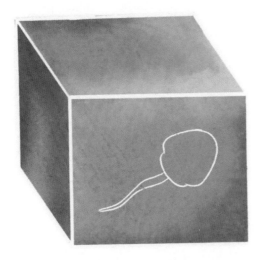
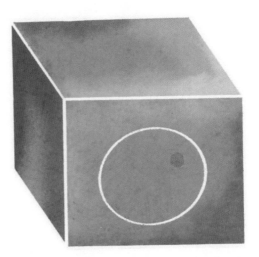

"Now," Mommy added, "every sperm and egg that come together have special instructions for how that baby will look, how tall they will grow and where all the parts should go."

"You mean... like blueprints?" Remy asked.

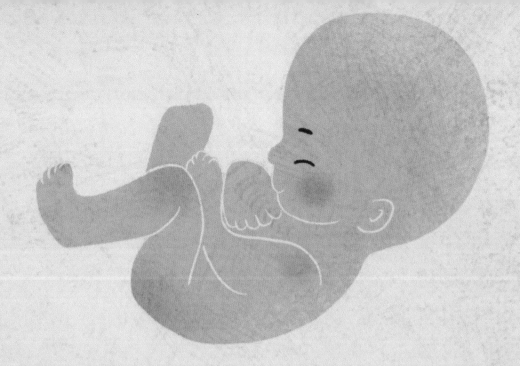

"Exactly!" said Daddy. "Or maybe we should call them 'YOU' prints!" Mommy, Daddy and Remy giggled.

"Sometimes you need other people to help you with the blueprints. You got some from the egg donor, like the color of your skin - and some from the sperm donor, like your wavy hair.

And, even though Mommy and I didn't give you our blueprints, we are still so much alike! You have Mommy's silly giggle and my toothy grin and we all love going to magic shows and eating ice cream."

"So even though I got my blueprints from the donors, my mommy and daddy are what built me!" Remy said with a big smile.

"Yes! We are so very grateful to our donors for giving us the blueprints to make YOU."

Remy began to play with her blocks again.

"But love is how you build a family, right?" Remy asked.

"That's right, Remy," said Mommy as she reached over and gave Remy a giant, warm hug.

Daddy put his arms around Mommy and Remy and made the hug even bigger.

Remy felt happy. She had learned that many families were just like hers.

"And if you ever have any more questions about the donors," Daddy added, "or even have any big feelings about our family story, we will always be right by your side so that we can talk about it."

"You know, Remy," Mommy said. "Daddy and I have helped build many homes. But none as special as ours."

Dedicated to the Jewish Fertility Foundation for their passionate work in building families - one unique story at a time.

With immeasurable gratitude to the donors, surrogates, medical professionals and scientists, who give so many intended parents a reason to believe in miracles.

To my family and friends for their unending support over MANY years who were - all along - helping me write the story I was meant to tell.

And for my most precious little girl. May your life be filled with joy and pride, in not only who you are, but where you came from.

YOUR FAMILY

DISCUSSION GUIDE

In these modern times, family building is no longer confined to the traditional means of the past. Families are being created with the help of cutting-edge science, and donor conception is an increasingly common and more socially acceptable approach to bringing children into the world.

As recipient parents, you are part of a new generation of families learning how to deal with delicate and ever-expanding topics like genetic family trees, ethnicity, and identity.

While it is encouraged to educate your child on the uniqueness of their conception, it's also just as important to remind your child that ALL children have a special story to tell about how they came into being - from conception to birth and beyond.

Kids are naturally curious and love to hear and learn about how they were created. This discussion guide is designed to help support the conversations you might have with your child about their story - after reading Remy's story.

Discussion Topic #1:
"Who is the donor?"

There is a wide range of curiosity levels from donor-conceived kids. Your child may want to know the donor's name and where they live.

Wanting to have concrete information about your genetic parent is very normal and integral to the development of personal identity. You can support that desire with as much information as you have about the donor/s.

Explain to your child that some people know their donors, some meet them later in life, and some never meet their donors. Some donors choose to be anonymous; to keep their identity private. Some donors agree to contact once the child is 18.

There is also a wide range of opinions among donor-conceived people about whether a donor should be considered a "real" parent. Many donor-conceived adults feel that it is important to not dismiss a donor as simply a source of genetic material, but rather allow them to be recognized as a "real parent" a "genetic parent" or a "biological parent."

Other donor-conceived adults feel it is perfectly fine to de-emphasize the role of the donor in the child's life and simply refer to them as a donor.

Though the answer you choose to give may cause you to feel complicated emotions, it is still crucial to allow your child to define family however they choose to do so - whether it's through genetics, love or both.

Discussion Topic #2:
"What do my blueprints look like?"

Your child may be curious about the donor's ethnic background and ancestry. They may ask whether the donor shares the same ethnic background as they do or ask about their heritage or race.

It is so important to validate your child's questions and let them know what you can share. Parents can explain how and why they chose a particular donor and include details about the donor's physical characteristics or ethnic background. You might find it helpful to create a notebook with personal details and photos about the donor to share with your child when you or they feel ready or even teach them about their ancestral culture.

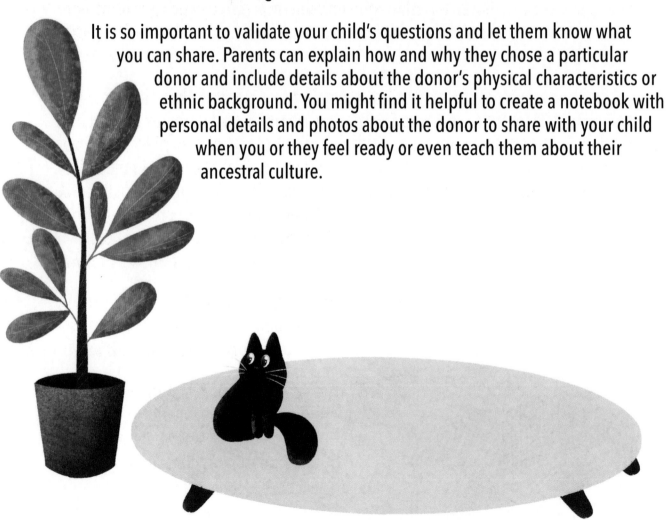

Discussion Topic #3:
"Does the donor know about me? Can I tell people about the donor?"

As parents, it is important to teach your child the difference between privacy versus secrecy. Secrecy connotes "hiding," which children often interpret as something that carries shame and negativity, while privacy allows for a person to decide for themselves when and if to share aspects of themselves with others. You can explain that their conception story is private, which means it does not have to be shared, but that they have a right to their story and to discuss it as they see fit. From a donor perspective, you can explain that donors often want to help others, but they also may be private about becoming donors and do not necessarily want to share their identity for similar reasons.

Discussion Topic #4:
"Do I have more relatives?"

It is very common for children to ask about other biological relatives, and this interest usually presents more in adolescence as children mature in their understanding of conception and genetic relationships. Donor-conceived kids are especially interested in half-siblings they may have. As parents, you can support, nurture, and normalize their curiosity. You can also form relationships with the families of their half-siblings through donor-sharing platforms, such as the Donor Sibling Registry, or by reaching out to your clinic.

The emphasis and central message for your child is how much they were wanted. As a parent, you dreamed, planned, researched, explored, and invested countless resources, all in an effort to realize your dream of creating your family. But also allow your child the space to feel any negative emotion attached to their conception story. After all, no matter how badly they were "wanted," a child might feel guilt or shame for experiencing resentment, confusion, or mixed feelings. Validate the normalcy of any and all emotions that arise.

Above all else, embrace your child's curiosity. While you have written the beginning of their story, the rest of the story is theirs to write!

Shubha Swamy, LPC, owner Novo Psychotherapy
On behalf of the Jewish Fertility Foundation
https://www.novopsychotherapy.com
https://jewishfertilityfoundation.org

Printed in Great Britain
by Amazon

29137777R00018